TIGRESS

HELEN COWCHER

ANDRE DEUTSCH CHILDREN'S BOOKS

The quick, sharp calls of monkeys in the forest sanctuary, warn deer that a tigress is near.

Outside the sanctuary, women come to gather firewood and herdsmen talk whilst their animals graze.

The tigress climbs with her cubs to the edge of the sanctuary.
She smells camels' breath and goat droppings wafting up from
the rocks below.

She leaves the sanctuary and pads silently through thorn
bushes, into the forbidden lands beyond.
Again, monkeys urgent, shrill voices fill the air.

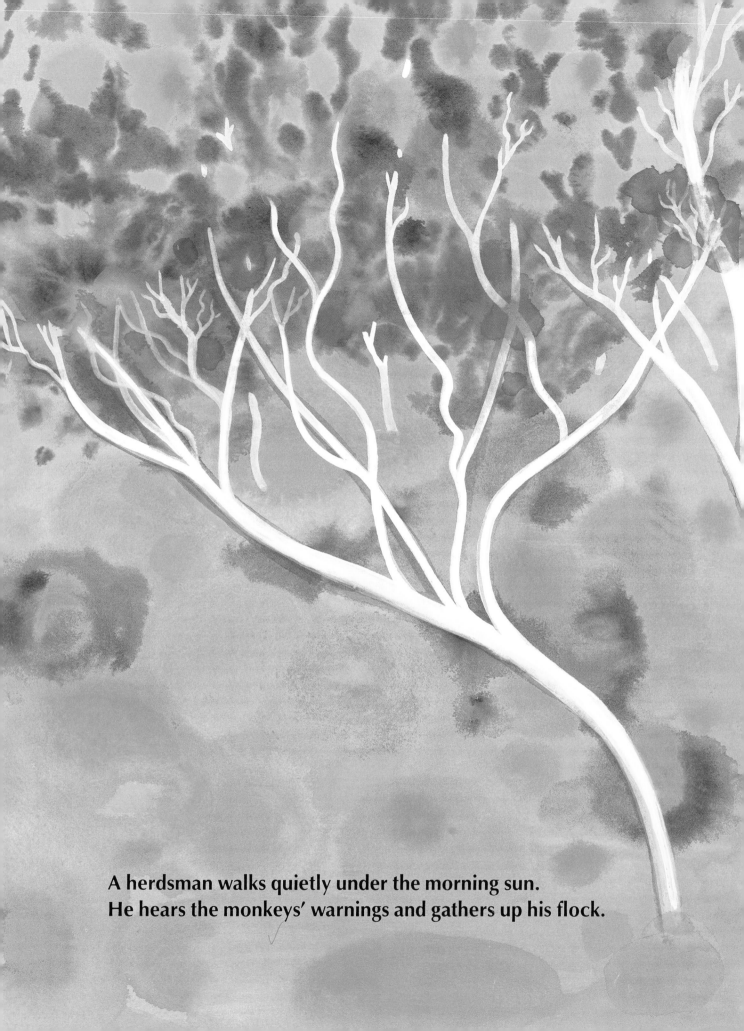

A herdsman walks quietly under the morning sun.
He hears the monkeys' warnings and gathers up his flock.

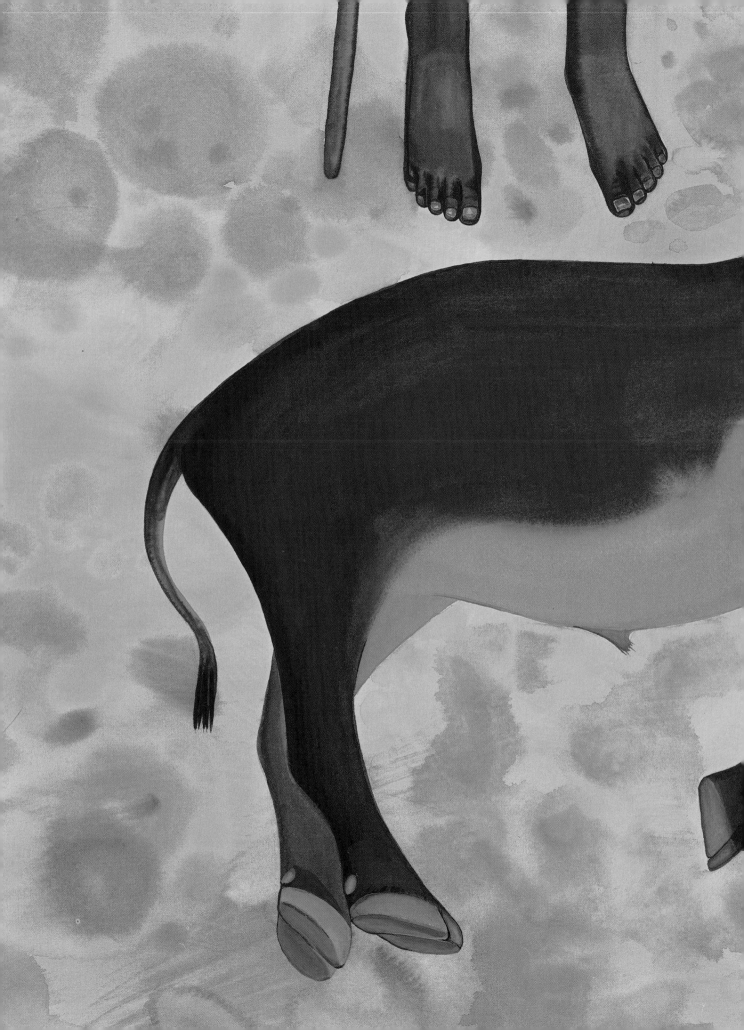

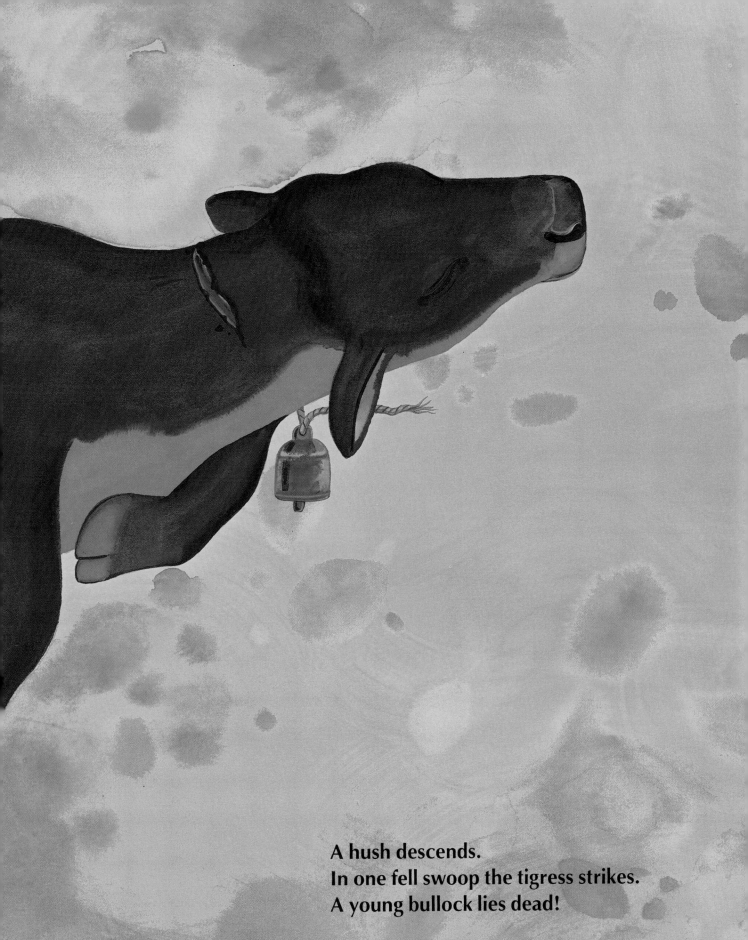

A hush descends.
In one fell swoop the tigress strikes.
A young bullock lies dead!

The poor herdsman cannot afford
this loss; nor can his friends.
He must warn them.

Meanwhile, the tigress drinks with her cubs at the waterhole.

Soon she will lead them back to the carcass to eat.

The herdsmen move their flocks;
goat bells jingle as they scramble
over the rocky hillside.

That night at dusk,
a stray camel is killed!

Around the fire, the cool air buzzes with anxious murmurings. Some herdsmen talk of poisoning the camel meat, before the tigress returns to eat.

The sanctuary ranger understands
the herdsmen must save their
animals, but he must find a way
to save the tigress!
Together they hatch a plan.

Later that night, the tigress returns to her prey.
Down wind lurk shadowy figures, silent and still.

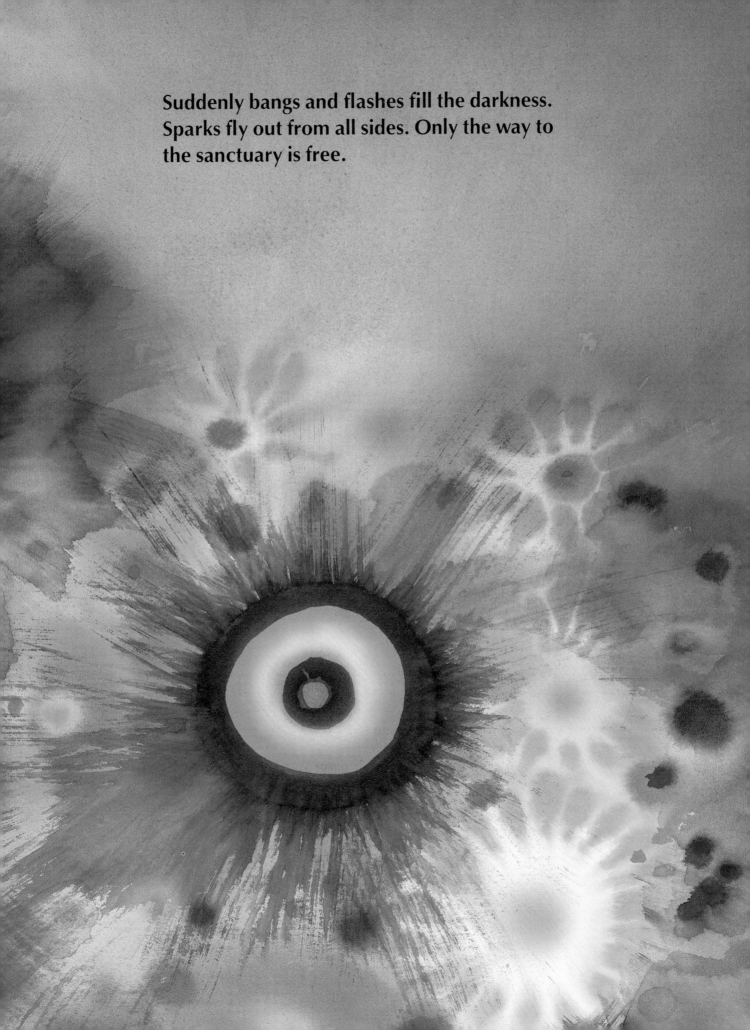

Suddenly bangs and flashes fill the darkness.
Sparks fly out from all sides. Only the way to
the sanctuary is free.

The tigress and her cubs are filled with fear.
They flee as more and more firecrackers explode
hot on their tracks.

As dawn breaks, they reach the sanctuary.
All is quiet and they can rest.

Beyond the sanctuary's
border, the scent of camel
and goat still wafts in the air.
The tigress twitches her
nose, then sleeps.